Look & Find
BIBLE

B&H
KIDS
EVERY *little* WORD MATTERS

Nashville, Tennessee

Toucan

Fish

Duck-Billed
Platypus

Crab

Chameleon

Lion

The Creation
(Genesis 1–2)

Grasshopper

Fish Eagle

Octopus

Frilled Lizard

Cow

Bee

Noah's Ark
(Genesis 6–7)

Noah

Mouse
& Carrot

Shem –
Noah's Son

Beetles

Noah's Wife

Ham –
Noah's Son

Meerkat

Japheth –
Noah's Son

Mason

Carpenter

Dog

Archite

Tower of Babel
(Genesis 11)

Donkey

Painter

Soldier

Cook

Soldier

Dromedary Camel

Goat

Dagon's Temple
(Judges 13–16)

amson

Delilah

Torch Lamp

Basket

Sculptor

Snake
Charmer

Food Seller

Angel

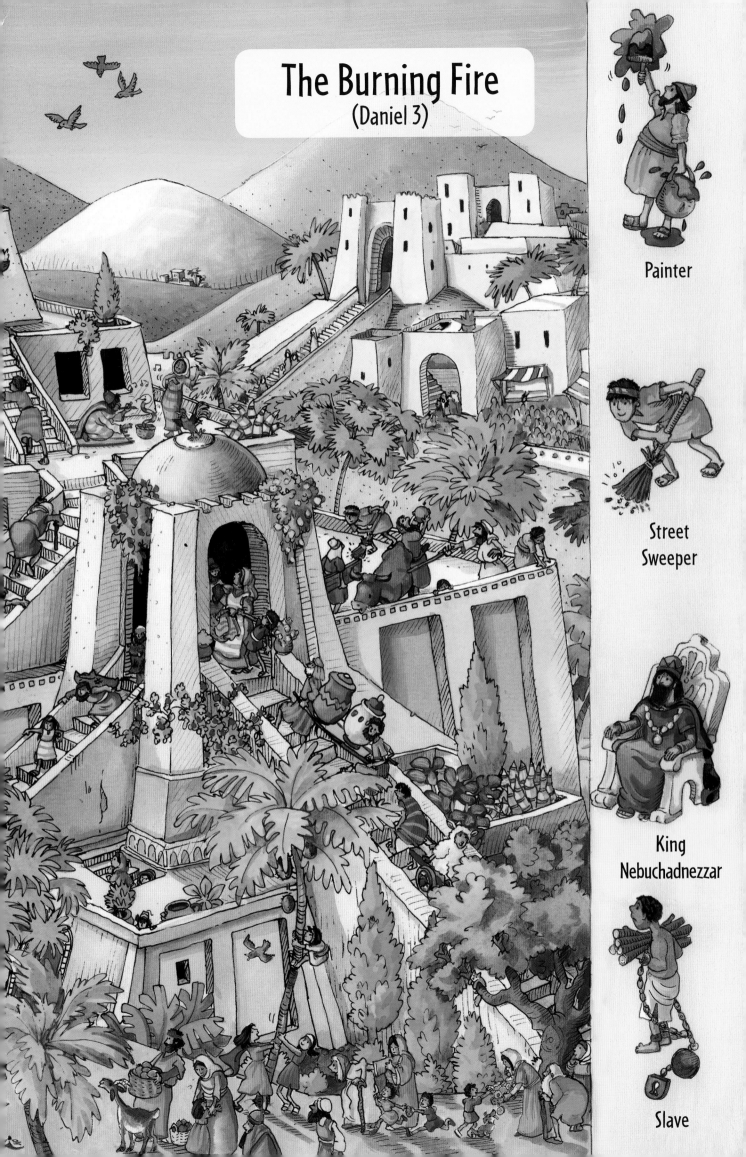

The Burning Fire
(Daniel 3)

Painter

Street Sweeper

King Nebuchadnezzar

Slave

Jesus Is Born
(Luke 2)

Donkey

Carpenter

Star Over
Bethlehem

Shepherd

Baby Jesus
& Manger

Innkeeper

Tax Collector

Roman
Centurion

Teacher

Carpet Dealers

Money Lender

Jesus in the Temple
(Luke 2:39–52)

Boy Jesus

Jewelry Seller

Joseph & Mary

Disciple John

Boat

Boy

Jesus Breaking Bread

Jesus Feeds 5000
(Matthew 14:13–21)

Basket

Disciple Peter

Boy Who Gave
His Little Food
to Jesus

Blue Bird

Jesus Enters Jerusalem
(Matthew 21:1–11)

Pharisee

Pilate

Little Girl

Little Boy
& Dog

Garments

Jesus

Easter & Ascension
(Mark 16, John 20, Acts 1)

Disciple Matthew

Angel at Empty Tomb

Sheep

Brown Goose

Jesus Ascends to Heaven

Boy
& Swing

Mary
Magdalene

The Cross
of Jesus

Burial Cloths
of Jesus

Sleeping
Soldier

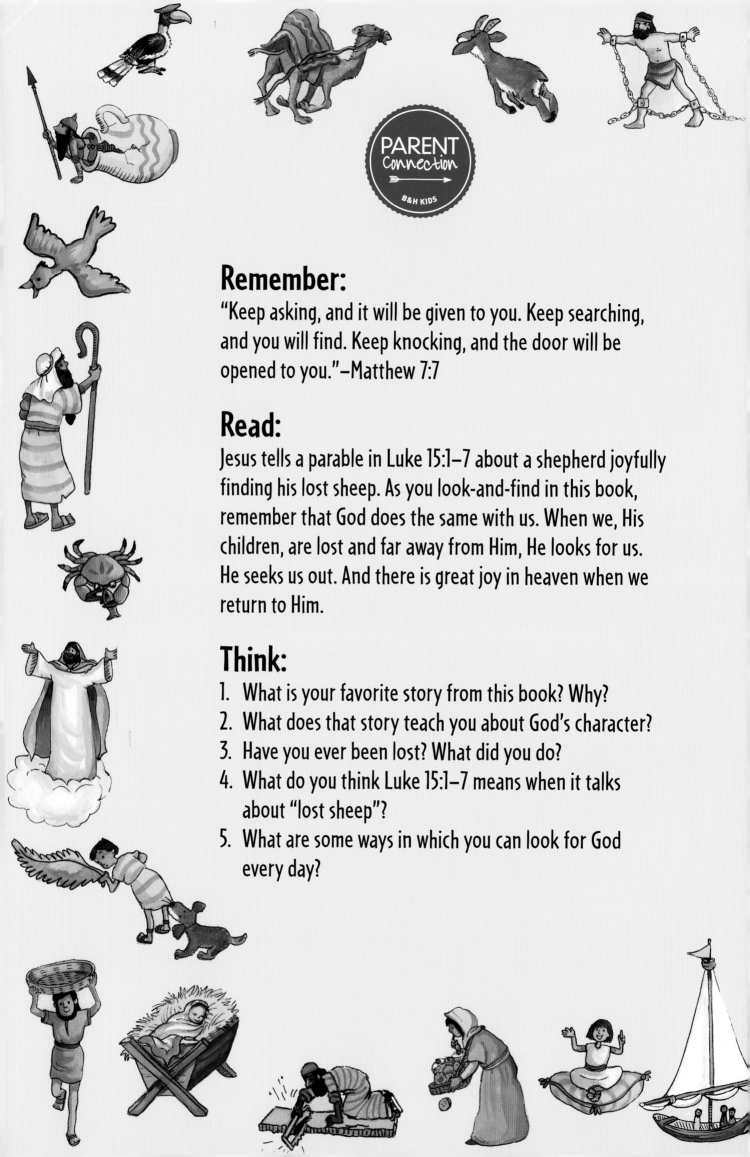

Remember:

"Keep asking, and it will be given to you. Keep searching, and you will find. Keep knocking, and the door will be opened to you."–Matthew 7:7

Read:

Jesus tells a parable in Luke 15:1–7 about a shepherd joyfully finding his lost sheep. As you look-and-find in this book, remember that God does the same with us. When we, His children, are lost and far away from Him, He looks for us. He seeks us out. And there is great joy in heaven when we return to Him.

Think:

1. What is your favorite story from this book? Why?
2. What does that story teach you about God's character?
3. Have you ever been lost? What did you do?
4. What do you think Luke 15:1–7 means when it talks about "lost sheep"?
5. What are some ways in which you can look for God every day?

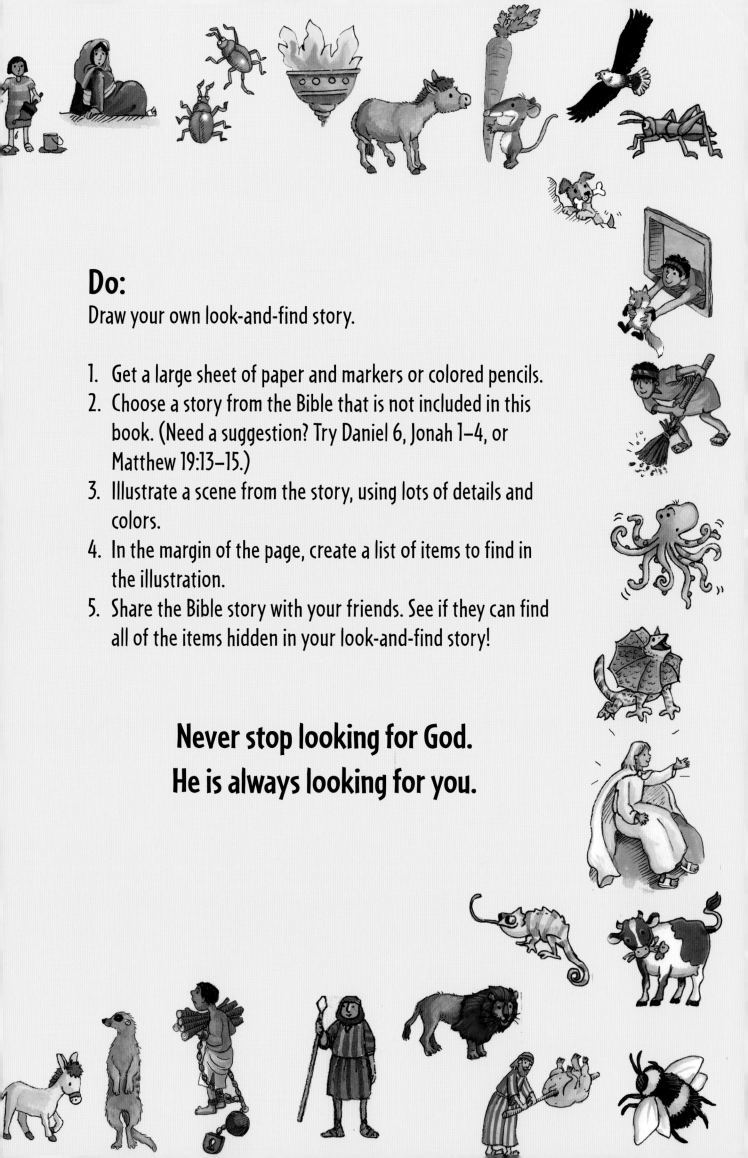

Do:

Draw your own look-and-find story.

1. Get a large sheet of paper and markers or colored pencils.
2. Choose a story from the Bible that is not included in this book. (Need a suggestion? Try Daniel 6, Jonah 1–4, or Matthew 19:13–15.)
3. Illustrate a scene from the story, using lots of details and colors.
4. In the margin of the page, create a list of items to find in the illustration.
5. Share the Bible story with your friends. See if they can find all of the items hidden in your look-and-find story!

Never stop looking for God.
He is always looking for you.

© 2014 by B&H Publishing Group
Nashville, Tennessee

ISBN: 978-1-4336-8262-9
Dewey Decimal Classification: J220.95
Subject Heading: BIBLE STORIES \ SALVATION \ CHRISTIAN LIFE

All Scripture quotations are taken from the Holman Christian Standard Bible®,
Copyright © 1999, 2000, 2002, 2003, 2009
by Holman Bible Publishers.

1 2 3 4 5 6 7 8 • 18 17 16 15 14